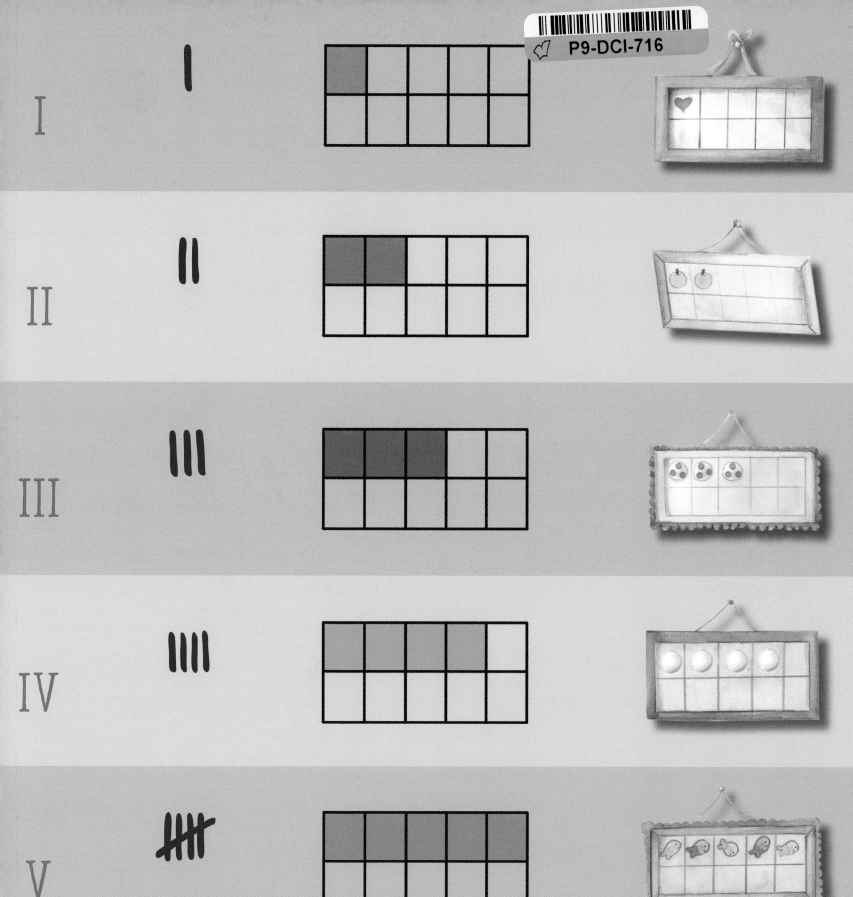

For Draco

Copyright © 2017 by Danica McKellar

Visit us on the Web! randomhousekids.com

Educators and librarians, for a variety of teaching tools, visit us at RHTeachersLibrarians.com

Library of Congress Cataloging-in-Publication Data
Names: McKellar, Danica, author. | Padrón, Alicia, illustrator.
Title: Goodnight, numbers! / Danica McKellar ; illustrated by Alicia Padrón.
Description: First edition. | New York : Crown Books for Young Readers, [2017] | Summary: Illustrations and simple text help the reader understand the numbers one to ten
and recognize them as they appear all around us, especially at bedtime. Includes note to parents.
Identifiers: LCCN 2015041117 | ISBN 978-1-101-93378-7 (hc) | ISBN 978-1-101-93379-4 (glb) | ISBN 978-1-101-93380-0 (ebook)
Subjects: | CYAC: Stories in rhyme. | Numbers, Natural—Fiction. | Counting—Fiction. | Bedtime—Fiction.
Classification: LCC PZ8.3.M45963 Goo 2017 | DDC [E]—dc23 | 2015041117

The text of this book is set in Harman Deco and Supernett cn.
The illustrations were created using watercolor and completed digitally.

Printed in the United States of America
10 9 8 7 6 5 4 3
First Edition

DANICA McKELLAR

GOODNIGHT, NUMBERS

illustrated by **ALICIA PADRÓN**

Crown Books for Young Readers ♛ New York

1
ONE

Goodnight, one fork.
Goodnight, one spoon.
Goodnight, one bowl.
I'll see you soon.

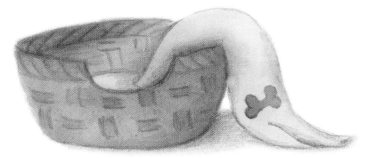

2
TWO

Goodnight, two hands.
Goodnight, two feet.
Goodnight, two ears,
so small and sweet.

3
THREE

Goodnight, three wheels.
Goodnight, three cans.
Goodnight, all trucks
and pots and pans.

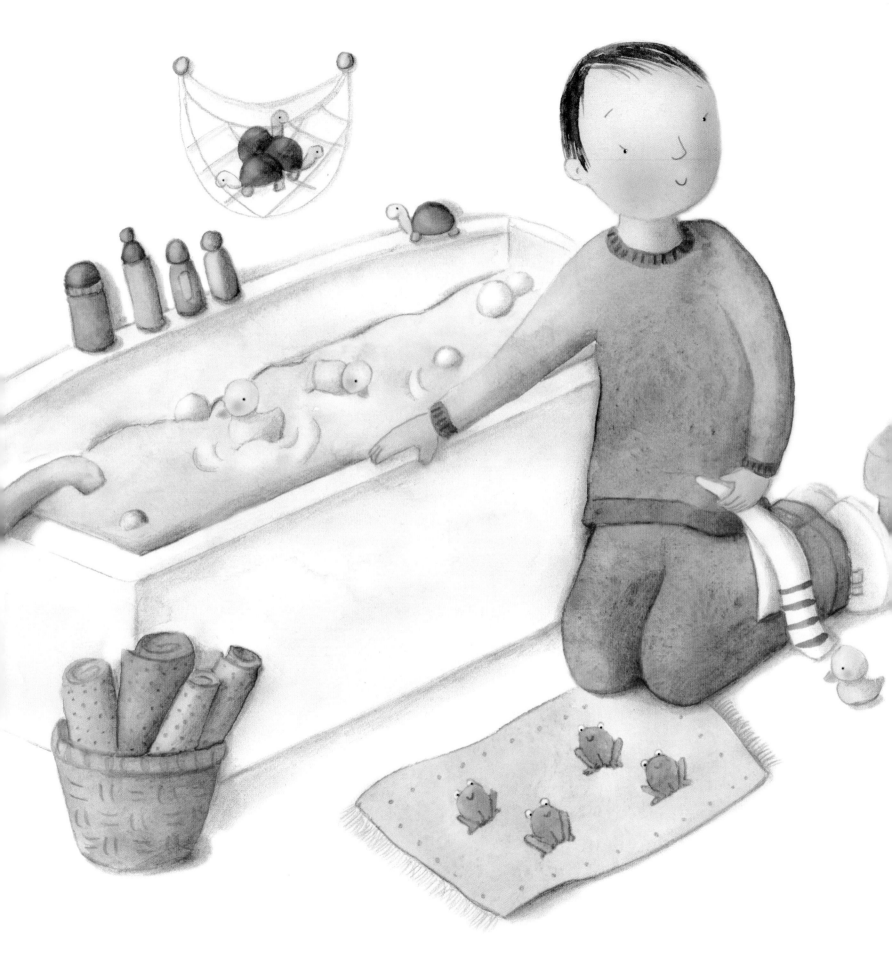

4
FOUR

Goodnight, four paws.
Goodnight, kitty cat.
Goodnight, four froggies
on the bathroom mat.

5
FIVE

Goodnight, five points.
Goodnight, little star.
Goodnight, five splashes.
They go really far!

6
SIX

Goodnight, six snaps.
Goodnight, Mr. Peach.
Goodnight, six blocks
with six sides each.

7
SEVEN

Goodnight, seven days.
Goodnight, whole week.
Goodnight, seven teeth
so clean they squeak.

8
EIGHT

Goodnight, eight arms.
Goodnight, tall vine.
Goodnight, eight sides
on the red stop sign.

9
NINE

Goodnight, nine butterflies.
Goodnight, nine bars.
Goodnight to the moon
and countless stars.

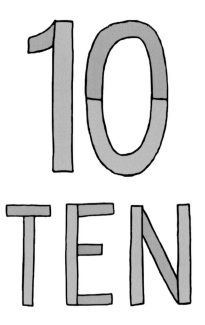

10
TEN

Goodnight, ten fingers.
Goodnight, ten toes.
Goodnight to the world,
and everyone knows . . .

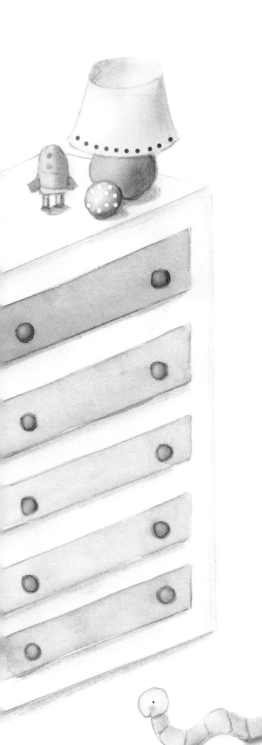

Numbers are around us,
like really good friends.
Goodnight to all the numbers.
Goodnight and . . .

The End.

Dear Parent/Grandparent/Caregiver,

Congratulations on putting your child on the path to a lifelong love of numbers!

As you probably know, there is an epidemic in our country of kids growing up learning to fear math, which of course can adversely affect their futures in countless ways. It begins at a very young age as they absorb the negative stereotypes surrounding math (that it's foreign, scary, not needed in real life) from the media—and even from family and friends. And with every day that passes in our increasingly tech-driven society, math becomes more and more critical for our children's success.

The good news is, we have the power to do something about it! And what is the solution?
Making sure our kids see math as "friendly" and relevant in their lives, and it's never too soon to start.

In GOODNIGHT, NUMBERS, each adorable spread shows its number *as it exists in the real world*—four paws on a cat, five points on a star, six sides on a block, etc. By reading this book every night, we are deliberately shaping how our children see math—as an approachable, integral part of their world.

So when you're at the grocery store, point out the unit prices. When you cook, talk about the fractions on the measuring cups. And when it's time for bed, read books like this one, where I've snuck math education into a story that feels like playtime. You'll be giving your child the priceless gift of confidence in math, helping to shape how the next generation of children see themselves their entire lives—as strong, empowered citizens who understand the value of numbers . . . and who certainly aren't going to let a little math scare them off.

How to Get the Most Out of GOODNIGHT, NUMBERS

- Point out that the *numbers* and the *names of the numbers* are two ways of <u>expressing the same thing</u>—for example, the number "3" versus the word "three."

- Look for what appear to be picture frames on the walls of each spread, and count the objects inside each one. These are actually "ten frames"—a teaching tool your child will see in early elementary school, which have been disguised as art inside picture frames in order to begin the process of familiarization.

- Look for other objects to count on every page! There are many to choose from on each spread.

- Take note of the endpapers at the very beginning and end of this book, which show many ways to express the same value—a fundamental concept throughout all of math. The languages on the endpapers are (from left to right): English, Spanish, French, German, and Mandarin.

- You can even show your child how the book applies to the real world. Point out the six sides on one of the blocks in your playroom, or count the paws on your pet!

- Come up with your own ideas! **Send them to me at *share@danicamckellar.com*, or find me on social media: I'm *@danicamckellar* on Twitter, Instagram, Facebook, Snapchat, and more!**

HAPPY COUNTING!

	English	French	German	Chinese
6	SIX	SIX	SECHS	六 LIÙ
	SEIS			
7	SEVEN	SEPT	SIEBEN	七 QĪ
	SIETE			
8	EIGHT	HUIT	ACHT	八 BĀ
	OCHO			
9	NINE	NEUF	NEUN	九 JIǓ
	NUEVE			
10	TEN	DIX	ZEHN	十 SHÍ
	DIEZ			